T0124442

Eclipsing Death

Michael Neno

AuthorHouse™
1663 Liberty Drive
Bloomington, IN 47403
www.authorhouse.com
Phone: 1-800-839-8640

This is a work of fiction. All of the characters, names, incidents, organizations, and dialogue in this novel are either the products of the author's imagination or are used fictitiously.

Published by AuthorHouse   03/08/2013

ISBN: 978-1-4817-8680-5 (sc)
ISBN: 978-1-4817-8681-2 (e)

Any people depicted in stock imagery provided by Thinkstock are models, and such images are being used for illustrative purposes only.
Certain stock imagery © Thinkstock.

This book is printed on acid-free paper.

INTRODUCTION

There are special times in time and space where it is possible to let your love concur the barriers between life and death to reunite the two parts of a love that has been untimely torn apart.

It happened for myself and Jane, the woman that I had loved ever since we first met as teenagers at school and started dating twelve years previously. These times only become apparent on certain days when the cosmic forces are willing to open themselves up and to let the spirit of a person whose soul is crying out for their loved one to pass from beyond the veil of death to visit their soul mate for a short while or be reunited.

It had been four months since the woman I loved died in a car accident while returning home after seeing some friends on the 11th of August in the year of 1998. After spending the rest of that year shut away from the world around me, in my sadness over the one that I lost, I was finally going to see in the beginning of the new year of 1999 by joining the huge crowds of revellers and remember the one I loved and lost so tragically on the 11th of August in the year of 1998.

CHAPTER 1

We first met when Jane joined my school in the town of Newton Priory after she and her family moved into my area of Devon where I lived from another part of the country. She was athletically slim with flowing wavy blonde hair and blue eyes, funny, caring; smart and all the things that guys dream their girl would be like. After being placed in the same class as I attended she quickly became the centre of attention to the other lads in it including myself; but not being particularly brainy, sporting or good looking I settled for just being there.

All through the final two years of school I considered myself right out of her league as she was never without a boyfriend be he the captain of the school soccer team or from a well off family financially and there I was not good enough for sport and from a family that was struggling just to make ends meet. Unknown to me at the time events were falling into place that would change things forever for both of us.

It all began when Jane was starting to be pressured by her boyfriend to go all the way sexually with him which she never wanted to so he began getting aggressive with her, with his popularity as a school sporting captain dismissing his behaviour. It was a Friday evening at the local youth club that things came to a head with them and I found myself drawn into their troubles. After drinking some alcohol which he had sneaked into the club Jane's boyfriend grabbed her arm and with her calling out for help amid the loud pop music being played dragged her into a small store room adjacent to the main hall as nobody took any notice believing it to be playing around.

At first I tried to ignore it, which was until I saw the tears that were running down Jane's face and the look of fear in her eyes which was when I knew that I had to do something about it. The screams saying "Leave me alone, get off me, I don't want to have sex with you." So taking a deep breath I followed them into the still darkened store room where the struggling by her to get free had already knocked some things off of some shelving and found the lad pulling and tareing at her cloths. Grabbing him by his shoulder I pulled him off her punching hard hitting him in the face with a well-placed right hook causing his nose to start bleeding. On hearing the noise several other guys came in and as I called out "He's raping her get him off." they forcefully removing him from the premises leaving me to place my jacket over her shoulders to hide her ripped top. The police were called and after only a matter of minutes they arrived arresting her boyfriend. After her very upsetting experience I found myself being the only one to comfort her. That night I walked her home and for the first time since she had joined my school and we talked enabling us to find an unexpected friendship.

The phones must have been busy that weekend because by the Monday morning the whole school was full of talk about the way that I had been a hero by saving Jane from her wicked boyfriend who had tried to rape her and how she had dumped him for me. She had dumped him that was true but we were not going out together. In the morning supported by Jane dressed in her school uniform an officer from the police and the school principle talked to the students about what had happened on the Friday night. Mr Smedly the principle announced the inclusion of an after school self-defence class which Jane was the first to enrol on. He also told everyone that her ex had been expelled and had been charged with sexual assault. And all that was until a couple of weeks later when after spending almost all of her time with me I plucked up the courage to ask her out.

It was whilst we were sitting in the school restaurant having a hot coffee after eating that I took hold of her hand across the table and said, "I know I've got nothing to offer a girl like you but will you go out with me?" "You've got more than you know to offer any girl and yes I will." Came her reply. That was enough for me but for the many sets of eyes that were scrutinising us it wasn't so Jane I think conscious of them leant across the table and kissed me fully on the lips causing my lips to tingle like they had electricity flowing through them. For her that was enough to let everyone know that I was now her guy and by the end of the day everybody knew it. "My parents know what you did to save me and I want to take you home so that they can meet and thank you." She said to me which I bashfully accepted.

During the final three months of our schooling the two of us were almost inseparable spending barely any time apart in school or out of it. On the most part we studied for our exams together but we did still found the time to kiss and cuddle whenever away from prying eyes mainly in a quiet corner of the school library and after school in the back row of the local cinema. The routine of studying Monday until Friday followed by going to the cinema or to a party on Saturday night was how things went for us until the end of our final exams and leaving school to join the world of finding work.

Going out into the grown up world and finding work although time consuming came relatively easy to us both. Jane having a perfect shape went into modelling and I acquired a position as a sales assistant in a large local retail supermarket. During the week Jane would be travelling around the country with her modelling while I was kept busy filling the shelves with goods for the store customers to purchase, but at weekends anyone could find us together. I found it incredible how a beautiful girl like Jane would wish to be with me but all the same just being with her made me feel special.

It was with Jane's prompting that on my seventeenth birthday I placed a deposit down on a 100cc motorbike with the money which I had saved over the previous ten months from my wages the intention being to ride that for a year to get a good road sense and then to buy and learn to drive a car. Another thing that happened on my birthday was the two of us became engaged making plans to get a small place of our own. Everything for me felt like I was actually living a dream, a dream so perfect in every way that I often expected to wake up but I didn't.

During the rest of March, all of April and the start of May Jane and I spent as much time as possible viewing properties for sale trying to find that special place to be our first home together. It was on Saturday May the eight 1997 that the two of us viewed a small one bedroom flat, built on the ground floor of Victorian brick building and being located on the outskirts of the local town fell in love with it quickly putting in an offer to buy it which was accepted and seven weeks later we were able to move in.

Michael Neno

On the fourth of July a Saturday we were given the keys to our new home and started to move our processions in. We spent the day unpacking our belongings and arranging the small amount of furniture which we had accumulated beforehand before settling down to spend our first night together. Because we had been so busy during the day with unpacking I nipped out and returned with a Chinese takeaway for our evening meal. It wasn't in any way that special but the bottle of cheep wine, soft music and a bunch of red roses made it quite romantic for us. Later Jane and I snuggled up on our couch to watch a video on the T.V and she moved herself closer and closer to me letting me know in my heart that I was the one she wanted to be with. Everything was feeling so good and right when suddenly she jumped up and rushed out of the room. "What's up, what are you doing love." I called out only to have her return moments later with a letter which she had written for me. Sitting back down beside me she handed me her letter which read

through good times and bad.

My friend, my buddy, Through happy and sad.

Beside me you stand, Beside me you walk,

You're there to listen, You're there to talk,

With happiness with smiles With pain and tears,

I know you'll be there, throughout the years.

When you want to ask the answer is YES. I love you now and always will.

I knew these were words written by another person's hand but the feeling inside of me became feelings of joy and contentment and so I took a hold of Jane's hand I reached into my trouser pocket and pulled out the engagement ring that I purched a few weeks earlier saying, "I know that we are still too young to wed yet but in my heart I know that you are my one true love, so Will you marry me when we're eighteen.?" Putting her hands around my neck she pulled me toward her and kissed me saying, "You are my love, my destiny and my future. YES I will marry you." That was a long time ago and yet it was still so fresh and crystal clear in my mind as if it was only yesterday, but it was so many months ago and I had to try and move on without her. This was hard for me as almost every day I would see or hear something and think, "Ah Jane will like that," I had to keep reminding myself that she was dead and try to get over her, but in my heart I still felt close to her. Every night I had nightmares about that terrible night when she was taken ever so suddenly from my side.

It was on the 10th of August 1998 when she kissed me after returning home from a model friend's house saying, "We're now both eighteen so let's book our wedding." These were words which I myself had been longing to say, so I without hesitation said, "We can do it next weekend my love" That was enough to bring a few tears of joy to her eyes as we got to our feet and we retired to our new bedroom to make love before settling down to sleep. While recovering from several hours of love making Jane looked at me and said, "As soon as we get married I want us to have a baby." I couldn't think of anything better to say other than, "Well stop taking your pill and let's start our family." Well what can I say other than we didn't sleep much that night or come to think of it we didn't sleep that much for a long time after that. On waking up the following morning I looked down at this beautiful woman in my arms and decided there and then that I would rather chew off my arm than wake her up. After the two of us had fully woken and got out of bed, dressed and eaten some breakfast Jane told me that she wanted us to visit her friend so that she could show off her diamond engagement ring to her that night to which I agreed. That was to be the last day we would be together. By the morning Jane would be dead, killed tragically in a car accident. I think a large part of me died along with her on that dark narrow country lane in the pouring rain. Even months later I found myself continuing to have flashbacks to that day, that is until my experience while at her graveside.

CHAPTER 2

With the memory of Jane was still so clear in my mind I promised myself to be at her grave side on the stroke of midnight to pray for her spirit. So at fifteen minutes before midnight, I put down my drink and departing from the party which I had made myself attend, setting off in the fresh cold damp air and set about walking through the thick mist that hung in the air toward the church where she had been buried four months earlier. Even then I was aware of a strong feeling of needing to be at her graveside on that night within me as if I was being called to attend. This was hard for me as almost every day I would see or hear something and think, "Ah Jane will like that," I had to keep reminding myself that she was dead and try to get over her, but in my heart I still felt close to her. Every night I had nightmares about that terrible night when she was taken so suddenly from my side. Things were made doubly difficult for me as with us not being married I did not get the needed professional help with coming to terms with what had happened.

Without the help and support of my family and friends I honestly believe that I would either have killed myself or been put in a straight jacket.

As I made my way along the quiet and relatively empty streets towards the church with my left hand holding my jacket collar close around my neck for warmth, my right hand holding a single red rose to place on her grave, my thoughts were of Jane and the happy times we had shared together. I walked along the loose gravel pathway and into the graveyard at ten minutes to midnight, past the 13th century granite built church and made my way along the footpath with the crunching sound from the gravel beneath my feet, towards the small willow tree which stood over Jane's grave and sheltering it from the elements so as to be as close to her as I could be on this night of all nights.

As I knelt down beside the last resting place of the woman I loved my thoughts were taken back to that night some months before when Jane and I had still been together and looking forward to a long and happy life together as a husband and wife. I can't explain what happened to me there but as I reminisced over the years that I was with her and that fateful night. I'm sure that out of the silence in the graveyard I heard her soft voice calling to me from out of the mist. "Mike my love, I'm here with you. We can be together again"

Straight away I jumped back to my feet looking around me for her but she wasn't there. Thinking that I had just imagined it in my subconcious mind I placed the rose which I had taken with me onto the top of her grave and with a tear in my eye and a heavy heart said "I'm never going to forget you my love." As the time reached midnight and the church bells started ringing out the end of the last year and new one in I could easily hear the sound of cheers and celebrations raising up from every direction as the world welcomed in the beginning of a new year and I wished that the one I loved was there to share it with me. My mind was filled with thoughts of the my Jane, whom I lost all those months ago, I could feel my heart seeming to cry out for the chance to be with her again and try to change what had happened. The trauma of what had happened was so great that I seriously considered killing myself to be with her but I did know that we would still be apart if I did.

Suddenly as if in answer to my hopes and prayers, I found myself sitting back in the car next to Jane, driving back along that same narrow country road as if time itself had been halted and turned back four months. She was in a joyful mood, happy after being hired to model a new range of womens summer dresses and wearing one of the new outfits home, a thigh length tight black dress that showed all of her curves. But why was I there of all places? was I going to be put through that same terrifying accident, or could I in some way manage to stop it from happening. I did not know. All I knew, I was going around the sharp bend that lay in the road and only seconds away, we would be struck by a farm tractor reversing out of a field gateway. And the car that we were in would be crumpled up and burst into flames ending the life of my one true love. Without even thinking about it I shouted out to Jane, "Stop! Quick Stop!" Jane pushed down on the brake pedal but the car carried on. We never stopped in time and just like four months previously, we rounded the bend in the road and we struck the rear of the trailer attached to the tractor. It was a living nightmare. The front end of our car folded in on itself pushing the steering column into Jane's chest making her cry out in agonising pain. I was catapulted through the windscreen and onto the twisted mass that was the front bonnet of the car in time to feel the heat of the fire that had ignited inside the engine compartment. Clambering off the mass of twisted metal that was her car, I made straight for the driver's door to get Jane out only to be met by horror.

In the driver's seat was Jane, her soft smooth skin hanging off her face burning. "JANE!!! Why must I go through all this again?" As I sank to the ground in pain and tears, wanting answers as to why this could happen and why wasn't it me there instead of her. But this was happening again and I knew she was lifeless. Yet Jane turned and faced me asking, "How much do you love me Mike?" and then, just like time had returned to normal, I was back in the graveyard beside her grave standing there in total silence and disbelief.

I could no-longer feel the cold air or the dampness of the mist on my face, it was like everything had paused around me and then it happened. Out of the mist appeared the figure of a beautiful young woman walking toward me with her arms held out in front of her and I recognised Jane just as I remembered her. She was wearing a long pure white satin dress with her long curly blonde hair flowing in the breeze, in a beautiful display.

Getting home again about 2am I was surprised when I walked into my front door by the sound of movement coming from my kitchen. There was somebody in my home, but all of my doors and windows had been closed and locked by me on going out. I tiptoed into my living room thinking that I had got an intruder and feeling around for something to protect myself with, my right hand touched onto a cricket bat leaning against the hallway wall, so I grabbed hold of it and moved as quietly as possible in the direction of my kitchen intent on bashing my intruder with it.

As I crept into the kitchen with my cricket bat at the ready I almost collapsed when standing before me I saw Jane. "What, what, what, what are you doing here!" I stammered in total shock and with quivering legs. "How did you get here? Why are you here?" were questions that I managed to get out before she stepped toward me opening her mouth to speak. "I'm here for you my love. No-one else can see or hear me." All I knew was that for a four whole months I'd not lived because when she had died in that mass of bent and twisted car wreckage I had also died inside.

With so much time being apart from her I wanted to take her into my arms and hold her again as I had done so many times in the past. Moving toward her I put my arms up ready to hold and kiss her but as I did so my hands just passed through her just as if she wasn't there. "We can't make physical contact yet, Mike. We have to wait a while but soon we will be able to" she said as my eyes looked at her as though I was searching for answers. For the rest of the night Jane stood as and I sat just talking until about 7 am when she said, "Mike. I've got to go. I have to go now because if I don't I will never be able to come back to you." With that she made a kiss to me with her lips and faded away.

To see Jane just fade away to nothing before my very eyes was hurting equally as bad as watching her coffin lowered into the ground some months earlier and as then, I was soon in tears. My only consolation was in her words where she said that she would be back and with time the two of us could be together again. There just one question going through my head that I was admittedly worried about Lindsey, a dark haired beautiful looking girl who had been Jane's best friend in life and had been a fellow model often working together while she was alive, could instantly tell that I was troubled by something. That evening, I invited her in so as to talk about the previous night's happenings.

As I related my previous night's happenings to her, she seemed to already be fully aware of it, as she too had a similar experience as I did. She told me how she had seen Jane in a dream and had been told how I could be reunited with her in time. I'm not a believer in the paranormal as a rule but I am open-minded to the possibility. So there was Lindsey and I, pondering how Jane could come back from the dead months after she had died.

The two of us spent the rest of the day together reminiscing over the years that along with Jane we had shared, which were full of fun and games, together until late into the night. At exactly 11.55pm the same time as the crash that killed her, we felt a sudden chill of cold air as our nostrils filled with the scent of Jane's favourite perfume and the large mirror that hung on my wall started reflecting an image of her sitting on the couch beside us. Linsey jumped up and I just froze where I was sat but not in fright, more in apprehension of who knew what.

There was no-one there but the mirror still showed Jane sitting beside us. Could this be a trick of the light or maybe I was seeing her in my subconscious mind. I couldn't say but one thing that made it real for me was Linsey could see exactly the same thing as I could. "What's going on Mike? Is Jane a ghost now? If she is, I'm not frightened." For the next ten minutes we just sat there as if glued to our seats and watched the reflection of Jane as it smiled back at us moving her lips as if talking. After some minutes the reflection of Jane faded away leaving

Linsey and I feeling totally at ease and for myself in particular I was feeling a certain excitment at the chance of getting her back and asking myself what I had to do to help her return to me.

Although neither of us spoke to others about this, over the course of the next few months I found myself drawn into a routine of having visitations from the spirit of Jane every night appearing in my wall mirror at 11.55pm, triggered off by the aroma of her perfume in the air around me. On a lot of these nights I asked Linsey if I was not going mad or having a mental breakdown in my sorrow. But with all this we were getting frustrated by not being able to talk to or hear her as she seemed to try communicating with us. This was upsetting for me as I could plainly see in Jane's face that she wanted to talk to me as she had done when first appearing to me in the graveyard the first time. Things carried on much the same into March when on the night before my birthday something happened which both surprised me and made me happy in a way that I hadn't been in such a long time.

It was, as I said, the night before my birthday and Lindsey had come around with a card and a bottle of wine to try and get me to celebrate this special day. I honestly never felt like it without the woman who I loved to share it with, but she managed to persuade me into having a glass with her which I did appreciate. One glass quickly led into another glass and that turned into another and another so by 11.55pm, when Jane's image appeared in the mirror, I was quite tipsy from the wine and Lindsey who was pouring it, was like wise just as inebriated as I was. "I've done what you asked me to do in my sleep last night Jane" said Lindsey trying to look sober. I felt as if it was the amount of drink that we had consumed, but I believe Jane spoke to me saying, "It won't be long until we can be together now babe. Happy birthday my love. I love you more than you'll ever know" before fading away this time into Lindsey as though the two of them were joining together. The arrival of morning found both Lindsey and I asleep, huddled up on the lounge floor, almost naked and both of us hung over from the previous night's drinking. I was the first to wake and on seeing our positions, I hurriedly rushed into my bedroom and quickly dressed while being aware of Lindsey.

"What happened last night I was out of it." was the first thing asked by Lindsey on waking and finding herself curled on the floor still half naked but I was finding it difficult to remember very much myself. I could however recollect some of what had happened and I was struggling to make sense out of it in my head asking myself if I had imagined it or if it did indeed happen as I thought it had. One thing that did weigh heavily on my conscience was the good feeling which I was getting having from this lovely young lady on my floor, something that I hadn't experienced since that dreadful night so many months earlier.

As I struggled to remember the night before, I questioned myself, whether her spirit was still inside Lindsey and why would she choose to do such a thing to me, letting me make love to her best friends body.

Closing my eyes I had let my mind wander back to the many occasions when I was in the same position with Jane but having felt Lindsey's warm body next to mine I couldn't help but kiss her fully on the lips saying, "I love you Jane, with all my heart." Before I had even opened my eyes again and returned to the present, Lindsey put a hand up to my face and kissed me back with the same love as Jane had, and very quickly things became intimate as I made love with Jane through Lindsey's body, but she was gone again and I had just been unfaithful without knowing or intending to.

After what had just happened I felt as though I had done something very bad by betraying Jane with her best friend but that wasn't all of it. As I lay face down on the floor afraid to move or even face Lindsey she stood up, stepped forward facing the mirror and said in a warm soft voice, "I'm so sorry Jane, I felt it all last night as well. Now I know why you want to come back so bad." As I lay there engrossed by Lindsey's actions it quickly transpired that somehow Janes spirit had merged with Lindsey's body enabling her to make physical contact with me. This happening put my mind at ease to a certain extent, but it did cause me considerable worry as Lindsey had herself experienced the whole thing, meaning that I had made love with her, as well as with Jane and that was to me being unfaithful. The only consolation to me, was to once again make love with Jane, but I had to via having sex with Lindsey.

Right through the rest of March, all of April and most of May neither Linsey nor I spoke of what had transpired on my birthday but we both knew that something had happened between us. I could tell that affection had grown within her for me and I would be a liar if I tried to say that she still held no appeal to me. Fortunately for me my love for Jane overcame the temptation to get that close to Lindsey again as they were like sisters before the accident anyway.

CHAPTER 3

Meanwhile with all of the things which were occupying my head I was unaware of the things that had taken a hold in Lindsey's mind. I was ignoring her and her feelings and was without realising it denying her the opportunity of expressing herself to me. I failed to even notice the way that after the night of my birthday in March, she had started spending almost every day that she was not away working with me, be it going out for a drink or just sitting in front of the television set and talking.

To most people who knew us the generally accepted thought was that I had finally moved on with my life by getting over my loss of Jane and was now dating her best friend. That in truth was not the case but under different circumstances, I would have been very happy if it was. Neither of us was particularly concerned about what others thought. No-body knew or would understand the things that had happened. To be honest I don't think that Lindsey or I really understood but we were happy with the idea of seeing my love and her best friend again. For myself I found it quite pleasing the way that a lot of male people started trying to be frinds knowing that both Jane and Lindsey were models, often asking if they did any posing for topless or nude magasines which neither did or wanted to do.

It was the end of May when I was dropped a bombshell by Lindsey. After having spent so many evenings together waiting and hoping for contact from Jane's spirit to inform us of when and how, she could return to life she confessed to loving me. It was not the thing that I wanted to hear as I myself was becoming confused inside about my own feeling for her. Yes, she was my loves best friend and yes, as such she had become a good friend to me, but my love was dead and Lindsey was a beautiful young woman plus we had already been intimate with tother, be it in the guise of Jane's spirit using her body to join with me in the act of love. I was starting to ask myself if I should try and forget Jane and get together with Lindsey, but each time I found myself questioning my own feelings, I remembered that night in the graveyard and the words of my loves spirit.

That night burdened with confusion and doubt I went out for a walk finding myself drawn without realising it to the grave of Jane, where in the cool air of spring, I prayed for help in my predicament.

As if in response to my prayers, like several times before, I found myself back in her car sitting next to Jane driving toward the inevitable crash that had taken her away from me all those months earlier.

Unlike the other times I just sat there quietly and accepted the inevitable outcome of what was to follow, but this time there was a noticeable difference. As we approached the bend in the road where we were going to crash Jane looked over at me and said something quite new. She told me in her soft voice, "It's almost the time my darling, keep your faith in me and don't worry about what is going to happen. I love you." With that we rounded the bend and smashed head on into the tractor trailer. As I felt myself being thrown through the windscreen I found myself suddenly back in the graveyard.

It was on the morning of the first Sunday of June 1999 the 6th that a knock on my front door signalled the time that was to test my trust and faith in a woman who was no more. Opening the door I was greeted by two large policemen who straight away said, "We are here to ask you to accompany us to the police station and answer some questions concerning the desecration of the grave of Miss Jane Thompson." Almost colapsing to the floor where I stood, "What do you mean? What's happened?" was my stunned reply. "It appears that last night person or persons unknown exhumed the body of Miss Thompson and we want to ask you some questions about it." was the explanation from the taller of the two officers stood before me.

Within only a couple of seconds I had grabbed my leather motorbike jacket and was in the back of a police car being driven to the station where there was a CID officer awaiting me to talk about what had happened. Still unsure of what had happened or why I had been taken to the police station I was getting quite concerned. I was shown into a small cell like interview room quickly being joined by the CID officer, who from first appearance, looked rather nerve-racking. I can plainly remember the feeling of unease and not knowing why I was there, but very soon I would know and all would become clear.

After introducing himself as DC Ammet, a big built, dark haired man with a look that could unsettle even a hardened criminal sat down at the desk where I was sitting and proceeded to ask me questions about the previous night's happenings. It soon transpired that at some point during the previous night Jane's body had been dug up and now all that remained was an empty grave with an empty coffin laid in the bottom of it. What I was not told was that her body had been dug up from the inside out. Had I have been told that then I would of known that somehow Jane had got herself out which in itself was amazing as she was definitely dead the year before.

"I know it was you. You were seen there by someone. Where is the body? What have you done to it? Why did you do it?" was the first of many questions. Yes I had been by her grave that night but I hadn't dug it up. I relayed it to DC Ammet who I doubt believed me. Hearing this news upset me greatly which I think the officer picked up on and he left the room, leaving me in my sorrow. Once alone, I cupped my face in my hands and broke down in tears. I was asking myself why someone would do such a horrible thing as dig up the body of a dead person and then I remembered.

I remembered the words of Jane's spirit in that I should keep my faith in her and not worry about what was going to happen. Suddenly as if all the sorrow and worry was being swept away from me, I began feeling as though everything would become clear.

On returning DC Ammet informed me that the forensics people had managed to find a very small amount of testable material by the grave which would enable them to get a DNA sample and until they had the results I would be kept in custody. He finished off by telling me that an officer would be bringing me a drink and something to eat a bit later and departed. All I could do was sit back and wait for the forensic results to come back.

Although I was understandably worried as to what was going to happen, I knew that I had not done anything wrong or bad, and time would show just that, but all the same, there was a part of me still worried that Jane's body had been dug up for some sort of bad reason. Within the hour I was brought a cup of tea and taken to a cell where I would have to spend the night. As I slept in my cell, which was about eight feet by six, that night my dreams were full of Jane and the time we had spent together before her death. It came as a great surprise to me when at 11.55 pm my cell filled with a bright white light and the image of Jane appeared from out of the wall and approach me as I looked over at her. In her soft voice she softly said, "I know you're scared that you are going to get into trouble for digging me up but there's nothing to be worried about, I had to be free from my coffin so I can come back to you." All that I could do was cry until she continued with, "When the full eclipse comes make sure you're at the place where I died and I'll be back." and with that, she appeared to turn and walk back through the wall just below the 12 inch barred window and above the bench that I was sitting on.

It was at 9.30am the following morning that DC Ammet entered the cell and said, "Will you tell me what the hell is going on with you and this Jane Thompson because I'm stuck here trying to solve a crime that can't be explained." I looked up into his stern face and asked what he meant by what he said. Sitting down beside me the officer opened a file which he was carrying, taking out the forensic report relating to the tests carried out on the material that were found at the graveside the day before,

He passed me a copy to peruse . . . She was pregnant but she had only just conceived. She couldn't have known that she was. As it was, it was mine and my pain instantly doubled.

Sliding the file back across the table top toward the officer he said, "There is no reason for you to be kept in custody for now, but if I find out that you're involved in all this in any way, I'll come down on you like a ton of bricks!. You are free to go but I would like you to look at this in case you can help us" I picked up and opened the report and quickly discovered that the fresh material discovered at the graveside was from a spot of blood found on the outside of the coffin lid. A fresh spot of Jane's blood had been found. Finding this out, though not that surprising, it was still a shock to me as almost a year after the accident that killed her evidence had been found proving she was alive only 24 hours earlier." Can I talk off the record to you Michael?" followed a nervous request from DC Ammet looking almost afraid to ask. "Yes sir, anything to help go ahead" was my reply to which he thanked me and then started to share his suspicions with me. Miss Thompson is still alive but I'm at a lost to explain it because the girl that died in an accident last year was positively identified as her. How can a person that was confirmed dead, be alive now almost a year later?" Pausing for a few seconds before continuing with," I get the feeling that there is something unnatural or supernatural going on here and I'm at a lost to explain it" and to finish off his statement, he said, "I've checked you out, so I know about the connection you have to this girl and I want to understand what's happening." I related to DC Ammet what I knew as he sat transfixed as he listened to my words, everything which had happened during the previous months, before allowing me to leave the cell that I was in and I left the police station to return home.

As I walked out of the doors and into the bright sunlit day I suddenly found myself inundated with questions from news reporters concerning what had happened to Jane and accusations of body stealing for sick reasons and cries of`` lock him up` and ` kill him` from others. Pushing my way through the hoard of people I felt a sense of not being alone. My heart started beating faster as although I couldn't see or hear anything, I was very much aware of not being alone. Jane, or should I say the spirit of Jane, was right there beside me. "I told you not to worry my love. Soon we can be together and we will never be parted again." echoed her soft voice from out of nowhere." Did you know that you were pregnant?" I said feeling incredibly proud and happy inside but saddened more by my double loss. I know, Mike, and our daughter can't wait to meet you. It's very important that you do what I ask you to do when asked." came her reply to me before seeming to go again.

She knew that she was pregnant and it was going to be a little girl but how could anyone have known unless in death she found out?.

Walking into the parking area outside I was met by Lindsey looking every bit the beautiful model radiating joy and relief at my coming out free, smiling with an obvious excitement at the news she undoubtedly was eager to share with me, we threw our arms around each other and hugged. Even before we had finished hugging she said with an air of excitement coupled with a little disbelief, "She's back isn't she?" to which all I could do was say, "I think so. Her grave is empty and tests have proved she was there alive yesterday, only 24 hours ago." She went on to say, "I've got to tell you something babe. It's important!" she went on to proclaim, so I suggested going back to my place so that we could have a drink and talk more.

As Lindsey and I started to walk along the pathway which led away from the police station we were stopped by DC Ammet calling to me as he approached almost running. As he reached us he said gasping for breath, "Look! I'll be honest with you. There's more to all this than you're telling me. I'm not after your blood here. I want to understand what's going on and I want to help if I can. I'm not talking as a police officer now so don`t think of me as one. OK. Call me John. I'm talking as just another man." I looked over at Lindsey looking for some sort of reaction to help me decide what to do and she just slowly nodded her head. So as we walked back to my place. We filled John in on everything which had happened over recent months as he listened attentively to every word.

After we had finished relating our story to John, he just looked at us open mouthed with amazement and bewilderment, unable to speak. Now it was time for Lindsey to tell me what had happened with her earlier while I was still in the police cell. "It was this morning when I was going into town to do some shopping. I was about to go and try on a new dress to wear out for a party when I'm sure I saw Jane looking at some lingerie in the next isle. When I looked over at her she looked, turned and looked straight back at me and lifted her finger to her mouth as if to say stay quiet. It surprised me so much I dropped everything and left the shop. I saw her again in the ladies when I was freshening up about half an hour later and she spoke to me." "What did she say?" I asked with excitement before she continued with "She just said to get ready for the eclipse and have faith and trust her." The forecast eclipse! I had been so engrossed with Jane and having contact with her spirit I had completely forgotten about it.

Looking at my watch I saw it was the 13th of June now meaning that the first incident at Jane's grave had been two months before the date of the coming eclipse, but to be honest I couldn't understand what the eclipse had to do with her returning from

Michael Neno

the dead. "If you've seen her, Lins's, then surely we have to find her now." I said almost in desperation. "No! It's not time Mike. The time isn't right yet for you." came her reply which made me go quiet." If anyone does it wrong the passage way between you two will be broken and she'll never come back. Not even her spirit and you'll need to find someone else to love. That much I do know" came Lindseys somewhat eerie warning." There is one private thing between us that I have to tell you later but it can wait for now."

While Lindsey and I shared her news with him, John just sat patiently listening in awe with his mouth open at what he was hearing, for a short while, before finding the words to ask a question." So if you don't mind my asking. What are you going to do now?" he asked, totally wrapped up in what he had heard. "What can we do?" I said, "It's obvious I can't do anything until August the eleventh and the eclipse. I just wish I knew what." I answered.

It was John who came up with an idea, that being to check the security camera's coverage of the shop, where Jane had been seen by Lindsey and have me make a positive identification of her just to confirm it was her and not a lookalike playing some sort of cruel joke on me. I agreed because I wanted to see Jane probably more than anyone.

Within the hour I was sitting with John watching the shops security camera footage, looking for the appearance of Jane. "There's Lindsey just entered" said John as we saw her entering the shop and walking along the main aisle towards the dresses, but I couldn't see Jane. We watched our eyes fixed to the action as she worked her way through the dresses taking some and holding them up against her and then putting them back. "So where is she?" asked John as we looked for her, but he saw nothing. For a good half an hour we were glued to the monitor, and then it happened. Lindsey had picked out one dress and was holding it up to her when we saw her suddenly look over towards the lingerie section where she had claimed to have seen Jane. We watched as she dropped the dress that she had been looking at on the floor and rushed over to the lingerie almost running before stopping dead in her tracks. She then appeared to be talking to someone for a few seconds before turning to rush out of the store. What we couldn't understand was the way that on screen there was nobody there which had us both confused. How could Lindsey have seen and spoken to Jane in a store where the security camera only filmed her. What we hadn't realized or saw was in the mirror on the wall used by customers trying new clothes against them was an image of Jane while in front of it was nothing.

We walked out of the store disappointed by what we had or hadn't seen, into the rain which had started while there. Looking up and down along the street we could see the public rushing from store to store as they were trying to avoid getting too wet from the heavy shower that had started as we ourselves walked fast to get back to my place where we could dry off and have a hot drink, neither of us sure of what was going on.

CHAPTER 4

"Well it's time for me to get back on the job, so I'll leave you to it. But do you mind if I keep up to speed on what's going on here as a friend. Not as a police officer" asked John reassuringly as he stood up from the armchair where he had been sitting. "Yeah, John, if you want to. But I'm not sure that I know what's going on here now. All I know is something is happening that I have no control over." As he walked out of my front door I turned to look at Lindsey as she sat there with a complete blank expression on her face and a look of bewilderment in her eyes. Moreso I saw a sign of fear owing to the presence of TV news reporters who had gathered outside wanting a story and answers to why Janes grave had been opened and her body stolen. One reporter, aiming his question at John, asked if I was being charged for what had appeared to have happened to which without answering he made sure that he could be seen shaking my hand and thanked me for my help with the police investigation. As he was leaving

John said in earshot of the press," I'll let you know if we find anything. Thank you again." Being heard saying that told the press that I was not a suspect or involved and the waiting press slowly dispersed. That sorted out I closed my door, and returned to Lindsey who was quite upset with everything said, "I know all this must have you so confused and scared but I do believe what you have said. I know there are things going on that nobody can explain, but we must have faith and allow ourselves to follow Jane's directions. Remember she was your best friend as well as my love." Saying that Linsey's eyes filled with tears as she replied with a shocking and unexpected statement. "I know Jane is always going to be the one you love, and she was my best friend almost like a sister but I can love you as much as she did and I am still alive." She paused for about a minute before taking a deep breath and continuing with, "I am in love with you Mike and want you to make love to me without her like that night when I let Jane use my body to make love with you. All I want is to have you for my own" Those few words should have been enough to set my alarm bells off but after the day's events I was not thinking straight.

I didn't know what to say to her statement because with it being so long since the death of Jane and having had Lindsey with me so much I had started to look at her romantically, but I had held those thoughts suppressed deep inside by telling myself it was just me desperately grabbing for a replacement for the love that I had lost. With that I did feel a need, but it was more than at that moment I could handle and very quickly we were wrapped in a passionate embrace and kissing with such passion. One thing led to another and before long we were laying naked in each other's arms touching and caressing each other. Then as if by magic I felt a sudden bout of guilt and turned myself away from her. We lay there me wrapped in guilt over what we had come so close to doing while at the same time wondering why I was feeling this way as there was absolutely nothing for me to feel guilty for. After all Jane was dead and buried whilst Lindsey was laid beside me naked wanting nothing more than to share and satisfy my sexual desires. We cuddled for a while before my coming to the conclusion that for us to become intimate would be completely wrong, so dressing again and leaving my bedroom with Lindsey still lying naked in my bed and clearly disapointed at coming so close to what she wanted.

As I walked out from the bedroom and into the passageway that led into the lounge I noticed a note lying on the floor by the front door so I stooped over and picked it up. Being late afternoon, I could plainly see it was not delivered by the post man, so taking it with me, I rejoined Lindsey who had got up and was sitting beside on my couch before opening the note up to read it. Reading it, I suddenly felt a deep sense of betrayal by me on Jane and my hands started to tremble. Seeing my anguish Lindsey snatched the note from my hands to read it herself. Once read she crumpled it up throwing it into the waste paper bin beside the couch.

"What do we do now Mike?" she asked after reading the note, "You know I can't keep it secret anymore and you know how I feel about you. I don't know what to do because Jane is and will always be my best friend, but why can't she stay dead so I can have you" Looking back at her I was confused as I myself had grown feelings for Lindsey but I had a much deeper love for Jane. "Well!" I said, "Its best we wait until the eclipse and see what may happen because it seems to be important." But what was so important about the eclipse I asked myself. Once Lindsey had departed I dug through the rubbish in my bin and finding the note to retrieve it. Taking it over to my couch I opened it out and read it again. I know you looked for me on the stores camera tape the letter said but remember you and Lindsey are the only ones who can see me for now. You'll need Johns help very soon because of someone we hadn't anticipated. The note was written and signed by Jane.

The eclipse was due on the 11th of August and it was still only the 15th of June so we had to wait for another eight weeks to find out what was going to happen. All I could do was hope that when the time came I would be able to do what was necessarily and not mess it up, more importantly, could Lindsey be relied on not to try anything to stop Jane from returning in an attempt to have me for herself.

I started to understand how famous actors and singers must feel having hords of followers loving them because of their talants. I knew that if Jane was still here Lindsey would not be the slightest bit interested in me as anything other than her friends guy.

Over the next few weeks, our time was spent looking everywhere for any sign of Jane but nothing until on the first of July when her spirit reappeared to me. It was during the night in a dream that I saw Jane standing in the road where she had died. The image in my head showed her just walk out of a cloud of mist into the light of day. One thing that did strike me as strange about it was the quick flashes of a calendar with the 11th of August circled and a time written under it. This was the exact time of the forecasted eclipse of the sun. That image stayed in my head even after awaking the following morning.

Once up and taking Jane's note with me, I went straight to the police station asking for D.C Ammet (John) who I knew would be on duty. An officer picked up a phone and called John who quickly arrived taking me into an interview room so as to enable us to talk uninterrupted. I handed him the note that had been slid under my door on the previous day which he read very scrupulously. After finishing the note he looked over his tidy desk and said, "If this note warned you of someone unexpected how do you know that you can trust me? After all I'm a detective that you've only recently met. "Because the note said that I will need your help when the time comes" was my quick reply. "So got any ideas of who this note warns you of?" was his next question, to which I had no answer. After several more questions we jotted down a list of four people's names that had any idea of what was going on. The names were the two of us Lindsey and of course Jane herself but there was a possible fifth who we simply called X. With my mind already puzzling over the X factor, John out of the blue started asking about Lindsey and my relationship with her. After reading the note again more carefully, John brought something to my attention that I hadn't even dreamt of before. "Have you considered the possibility that the note may not even be warning you of an unknown person, but perhaps someone you do already know` X` and they will do something unanticipated? Say maybe Jane's ex-boyfriend. I know that he is serving time for his assault on her and it was you that stopped him, or maybe it refers to Lindsey and her feelings toward you. From my past, women can be very devious when it comes to matters of the heart;. Either way I'll make some enquiries and let you know if I turn anything up." With that we said our goodbyes and I left the police station heading home still thinking of the notes warning and of course Lindsey.

Once back in the quiet of my home I made myself a drink sat down, and thought for a long time about Jane, myself and Lindsey and where we all were in everything that was happening. I had fallen asleep by the time that night, and right on schedule, I became aware of Lindsey coming through the front door. The first thing she did was to kiss me very passionately and tell me how much she had missed me that day and how much I would have enjoyed being on her days photoshoot because it was for lingerie for a mail order catalogue. It felt as though she was acting like a loving wife, partly my own fault because with everything that was going on, I had given her Jane's door key so that she could let herself straight in. Trying hard to ignore my attraction to her I did my best to avoid any sign of flirting by her, while talking about Jane and fixing my attention on the T.V set. It was about nine o'clock when the phone rang and it was John on the other end checking if I was home because he had some information for me. When I told him that Lindsey was here, he came to the flat. I made him a drink and sat down to listen to his news. He started by informing me that David (Jane's ex) had been released from his incarceration and was currently living with his new girlfriend. More than that was his girlfriend had asked associates about Jane and I why that was, was unknown so he was definitely still in the running as our mysterious X. So too was Lindsey, because she had been heard telling a work colleague that she wanted and intended to make me hers within as short a time as possible, although that was unconfirmed. Hearing this did make me feel somewhat uneasy but I knew that while she was still alive the two women had been like sisters but there was the night that Lindsey had felt everything when Jane used her body so as to make love with me again. Maybe Lindsey thought that I was making love with her and my feelings had changed. Before he left, I opened myself up and told John everything which he took in astounded and I think somewhat flabbergasted, and to have actually spoken with her but again nothing has been confirmed." Not knowing just what the time was right then, you could of knocked John down with a feather when out of the mirror that hung on the wall came a cloud of mist like water seeping out of a spring and out stepped Jane.

After composing himself John stammered in the best friendly police man voice he could, "So you must be the elusive Miss Thompson that has been causing such a mystery around here." Before either of us could speak again Jane replied with, "Yes I am Jane and I am very pleased meet you John, you're a good man." "How do you know my name? I've not told you." he responded to her answer. "Here we know everybody's name, now listen to what I can tell you because I don't have much time left." came Jane's next statement which had both John and I rooted to the spot where we were. Having our full attention she continued with what she had to tell us. "It's almost time for my return but I need both your help. Lindsey's life depends on what you do because she is about to receive some very bad news."

That night I could not sleep with worrying about Lindsey, her eyes sore from crying and an unsteady stance. "Oh my God, sweetheart, what is the matter?" I asked, half expecting the news that Jane's spirit had warned me about the previous day. I was deeply saddened when she revealed that she had just returned from the local hospital where she had an appointment with a consultant who had informed her that she had cancer, bad news in itself but much worse because it was grade four breast cancer meaning that she had little time left to live maybe only months." Will Jane be on the other side and will we still be best friends like before? She asked in a frightened tone, trying not to cry before adding something that made me question myself. We talked until quite late about what was left of her life, how her parents and little brother would react knowing what would happen to her. Her last comment before falling asleep was going to stay with me for the rest of my life. She said "Why can't I take Jane's place with you and let her stay dead until I die." At that moment I would have very happily of done just that if she could be better again, but how could I turn away from Jane and everything that she meant to me.

After another sleepless night mulling over all the things that the previous night had revealed to me, I knew that I needed to see or at least talk with Jane. As so many times in the past, at 11.55 pm Jane's spirit appeared to me from out of the wall mirror, in my lounge and let me know everything that had already happened that day. She could easily understand Lindsey's situation and wishes which was to lead on to what was to happen later." Is there anything that I can do to save her? I asked desperately not wanting to lose her from my life as well." No, nobody can do anything to help her yet, but be comforted because in a very short while she will be well and we can all be together again just as we were before I died. I know this my love, so don't fret." We were able to talk a little more before she faded back into the mirror again, leaving me more at ease but not able to say a word to Lindsey.

I made the decision to let Lindsey know nothing of it while playing along with her wishes so as to give her some happiness during her last days. That would be difficult to do while staying faithful to my Jane but at least I only had ten more days to go until the eclipse. As it turned out that was relatively easy that is until the Sunday before the eleventh when after a late night at the local club with her I woke up to find out that I had not returned home but was at Lindsey's place and in her bed with her. I remember asking myself what I had done. Had I spent the night having sex with her, I wish that I could remember what happened and why I was in the wrong bed lying next to the wrong woman. I managed to slide out of bed and dress before I sneaked from her room and left, going home and feeling very guilty over what I may have done the night before.

With only four more days to go before the eclipse and Jane's return from the grave, I had the feeling of guilt over my night with Lindsey plus there was so much yet to do in preparation. I had not seen anything of John in over a week so I felt that I should contact him and check on preparations. After leaving a message on his answering machine I was just about to get myself a shower when I heard the sound of her coming in. Lindsey's made me nervous about what she might say or do. I opened the bathroom door only to be greeted by, "What the bloody hell happened to you last night? I got you drunk to get you home and make love all night but what did you do. You threw your guts up and crashed out. It took me ages to get your clothes off and into bed. And when you left this morning, why didn't you wake me to say goodbye?" Feeling my guilt over the night before lifted I quickly responded with, "I'm very sorry. I must have drunk more than I should have and I can't apologise enough for being so sick." The telephone ringing gave me a reason to go back into the lounge, it was John on the phone, who hearing her in the background just said, "Can you come to the station his afternoon because I need to ask you a few more questions concerning Miss Thompson."

That afternoon dressed in cut-off jeans and a T-shirt I walked to the police station alone where John was waiting for me. "Good you haven't got you know who. with you. We have some important things to discuss and I don't want her knowing about them." he said in his official detective voice, I think as much for himself as me especially after his first contact with a ghostly Jane. Once in his office he could talk to me more freely which he very quickly did, starting with, "About Thursday I've managed to get the stretch of road you are going to require closed for several hours but any longer will cause serious problems. That was one potential snag sorted out now there were more to make sure of Lindsey. "Now as for Lindsey, we had to come up with an excuse to firstly keep her away from where I would be and secondly stop her from interfering in any way. That would be a problem so we decided to think it over for the next couple of days. Before leaving him John told me how he had written a letter to himself with a photograph holding a newspaper with the date showing as confirmation detailing everything and would give it to me on the Wednesday night. With only that night, Tuesday, Wednesday and Thursday to go I could really do with some help in finding a way to get rid of Lindsey for the eclipse.

That night as if in an answer to my prayers, Jane appeared to me in my bedroom. As if she already knew what troubled me she said, "I think I should use Lindsey again so we can make love like before." "But she will feel it too. And you will experience me being unfaithful to you." I replied to which she came back with, "But for her after the eclipse it wont have happened so how will she be able to remember something that hadn't happened yet for her and besides it may be her body but it will be me that you're making love with." Thinking of it that way it was a good idea but that still left me knowing that I had made love to another and I still had the problem of how to get away on the Thursday. Bearing that in mind, I was able to face Lindsey on the Tuesday without worrying too much about what she may do.

As it was the Tuesday came and went with relatively no problem until the evening when a couple of things happened. First came a visit from John about seven o'clock handing me a letter addressed to himself asking me to personally hand it back to him after Thursday's eclipse, and secondly he told me not to appear seemingly excited when I explained that I had a visit from Jane's spirit the night before asking her if she could share her body again to have sex with me. Knowing that I had already arranged it with Jane, I pretended to be surprised but went along with it. Later on, when Lindsey arrived, I said "We will have to wait until Jane's spirit shows before we can make love" when Lindsey came back with, "Why wait for her? I can please and love you." "No" I said "If we are going to be together and let Jane stay dead I think it best she has one last chance of being one with me."

It was plain for me to see that she wanted me for herself, for the little remaining time that she still had, but I wasn't going to give up on Jane even though it could be so easy to do so by just not being at the place that she died and letting her soul go forever. No, I wasn't going to give up that easily. We had shared so many trials and tribulations together, to conveniently simply let her go, bearing in mind the fact that if Jane had not died then Lindsey would not even be attracted to me, plus I do not believe that could I cope with losing Lindsey to cancer if nothing was done.

I made an excuse and left Lindsey in the lounge watching the T.V while I went to my bedroom where I called John and asked what he had planned for picking her up" Now I knew what I had to do but how could I keep her busy until morning. "Why are you coming for her?" I asked to which he used the excuse of taking her to a specialist who might be able to treat her very serious condition. As far as she would know he had been using the telephone and calling in favours from people he knew to get her the help that she would be needing over the time that she had left. This news gave me an idea so on returning to her I crossed my fingers behind my back and made a commitment to her that would deminish the risk of her spoiling things the next day. "Lindsey. I've been doing a lot of thinking and have decided that I want to marry you and forget about Jane." With that news her face lit up like a christmas tree and swung her arms around me saying that she wanted to tell her family and friends straight away and move in with me as soon as possible. I just hoped even prayed that Jane knew and agreed with my actions knowing that in 24 hours all this would never have happened.

With Lindseys condition draining her of energy and zest for life I told her to stay with me that night and we would visit her family the next day to give them the good news, but for now she should lay down and try to sleep which she agreed with, so carefully I walked her into the bedroom and laid her down. Later,. I heard coffee being stirred by Jane to let me know that she was in the kitchen and wanted to see me so I sat myself down on the couch only to find my bottom landing in a car seat right next to Jane. This time unlike so many times in the past we were not driving head long into the inevitable crash but was stationary. "What's happening?" I asked in total surprise. "Do you trust me asked Jane? to which I answered ""With my life." "When its time, avoid being near Lindsey because she thinks you want to be with her and I will not come back." "I know. Its tearing me apart letting her believe it, she never would if I were still here and her best mate." "No, and if everyone does what is needed I will still be here, alive and with you all again." reassured Jane, making me feel confident of my future. In the blink of an eye I was again sitting on my couch. At this particular time I wanted so badly to tell Lindsey that she was not going to die of cancer as a sort of reward for her help in allowing her deceased best friend live and love again but if I did there was no guarantee that she wouldn't do everything to prevent things happening as planned.

For now I had to avoid anyone and anything that could prevent my being free for the eclipse. On the evening, I was nervously pacing, and rushed to the window to see how bright it was outside but we had total cloud cover which had me worried that the eclipse not being visible might obstruct my being at the right place and at the right time. I need not have been concerned as the eclipse would still happen and my Jane would, before long, be with me again. Getting dressed quickly I made myself a cup of tea and picked up the telephone and called John to confirm that he was indeed keeping Lindsey busy and the stretch of road needed clear to which he told me yes and wished me luck on the day. With a quiet confidence and a spring in my step I walked out of my or more like `our` home and leisurely strolled down along the road outside which joined onto the main road into the town where the crowds of people were looking for their best spot to witness the upcoming eclipse. Stopping every few metres and looking upward at the clouds while asking myself, was this for real or was I about to wake up and find out that nothing had changed and I was only dreaming. I didn't even notice a group of three of my neighbours trying to attract my attention to invite me to join them in their eclipse watch. And then it happened, just as I reached the spot where a year before I had lost my everything I was back in the car sitting next to Jane driving along the road toward the inevitable crash, but this time, I was able to press the brake pedal just in time to avoid hitting the tractor trailer that was in the process of reversing back out of a fields gateway. This time she was not only wearing the same designer dress that she was modelling, but just like the year before it was raining and I knew that this was what I had been dreaming of. She looked over at me and said in a grateful way, "I knew you would save me and bring me back my darling, now everything should be back a year and we have an eclipse to look forward to."

This time anticipating the prayed for return of my Jane everything appeared to freeze stationary, even the falling rain was suspended in mid fall and the gusty wind had stopped. I could have been in a picture, what was going on around me? Then I heard it, a voice so heavenly and comforting that I could not think of it as anything other than God. He informed me that Jane would indeed return to life but for her soul to come back another would have to take its place. Ordinarily I might had chosen Lindsey to take her place but I couldn't. Both girls were special to me with their whole lives ahead of them even though Lindsey was suffering a cancer that would kill her. Straight away I knew in my heart that I could not be the instrument of deciding who had to die for Jane's return and without thinking about it I just offered to die for her so that two beautiful people could have their rightful opportunity of life. "You are willing to give your life freely for another, are you sure this is what you want?" he asked, to which I said yes. "I knew that you would decide in that way, but I needed to hear it from you before I allow this miracle to come about." And then, everything was happening just as we had been preparing for during the last year. The rain started falling again and the wind was gusting again, more than that Jane was alive and I had not died, even Lindsey wouldn't even die. All was well in the world again.

My beautiful Jane was alive again and back at my side where she wanted to be but I was still aware of everything that had happened during the previous twelve months that now had not happened yet. More than that I knew that she was pregnant with my child or was she? And what about Lindsey and John they both knew what was going to happen but would they remember because for them it had not happened. "Let's go home now my love and celebrate my rebirth." Said Jane to which I agreed. "Seeing as we have twelve months to relive maybe we should spend them in bed having sex" I came out with to which Jane's reply was, "mmmmmmmm that sounds good to me." showing the same warmth and love that I knew and loved along with a very sexy twinkle in her eyes. Yes, my love was back.

One thing that I had completely forgotten about was the x factor person, who was it and why were they a threat to Jane's returning. On pulling up outside of our flat the look of relief, at coming home, on her face was a picture that I will always treasure. We entered our flat and straight away flung our arms around each other and kissed like never before as we started to undress each other to make love. After a long night of passion and a late breakfast I surprised Jane when from out of my jacket I pulled out the sealed letter that John had given me to hand to him after the eclipse.

Opening the envelope she pulled out firstly a photograph of her opened grave and a hand written letter describing everything, plus another photograph of him holding a copy of a national newspaper showing the day's date now in a years' time. "You cannot give this to him or our lives will become the topic news stories everywhere, and we don't want that." She was obviously right so finding something to light it with I burned it all. Now we could get on with our lives just like everyone else and what happened would become nothing more than a story, but first I wanted to visit the graveyard and see the spot where her grave had been.

As we walked up the pathway toward the church and it's well looked after graveyard Jane wanted to know how much of the coming year I remembered because she was hoping that we could book our wedding for a time that we knew the sun would be shining for us. As we reached the right spot we saw that there was an empty space where Jane had been buried, the sight of which brought tears to my eyes as I remembered the pain and upset that I had endured. So far everything was turning out perfectly but there was still one person who I needed to see and check on, Lindsey so Jane borrowed my mobile phone and called her to invite her out for a drink that night. During that evening mainly the girls talked about whatever girls talk about, fashion, music, movies and of course boys but my heart almost missed a beat when Lindsey started telling Jane a dream she had where she had died and come back to life during the eclipse that had just occurred. "It was so real that I seriously believed it actually happened but it couldn't have, could it."

WOW, Saved by acceted scienctific knowledge and refusal to believe in miracles and the possibility to the wonders of true love.